Capture of the Twin Dragon

Anthony G. Bollback

Capture of the Twin Dragon

COVER ART BY

www.curraheegraphics.com

ISBN 978-0-9849359-1-8

Printed in the United States of America

Published by

www.FindingChristBooks.com

DEDICATION

In memory of my parents,
Anthony and Elizabeth Bollback,
who led me to Jesus through their prayers
and godly lives.

Table of Contents

Off to Hong Kong....1
The Perfect Crime....7
A Trip to the New Territories....15
An Unexpected Discovery....23
The Secret Door....36
Caught!....47
The Search....54
Attempted Escape....61
Discovered....72
A Night on the Twin Dragon....80
Escape in the Dinghy....94
The Escape Discovered....108
Safe at Last....126
Parting News....135
Would you like to know Jesus?....140
About the Author....143
Books by Anthony Bollback....145

Chapter 1

Off to Hong Kong

"There's a mystery waiting for us in Hong Kong," Jack whispered to his twin sister seated by his side on the Hong Kong bound plane. "I feel it in my bones," he chuckled softly.

"Better not let Mom hear that," Jenny whispered with a twinkle in her eyes. "Remember, she said the memory of our last trip and the capture of the jewel thieves was enough to last her a lifetime."

"I can hardly wait to see Tim and Ruth again," Jack said with a wide grin. "It's been almost a year since we said goodbye to them, and I bet they're ready to take on another mystery, too." He glanced out the window at the white fleecy clouds far below and smacked his lips with satisfaction as imaginary thoughts of smugglers hiding in those clouds raced through his mind.

"I just feel it in my bones," he repeated with emphasis. "There's got to be something special waiting for us to solve." Jack settled back in his seat, closed his eyes, and drifted off to sleep. He was suddenly awakened by the voice of the captain announcing that they were about one hour out of Hong Kong.

"I had those thieves on the run," he said ruefully as he awakened from an exciting dream. "I only needed a few more minutes and I would have captured them!"

"What are you talking about, Jack?" his mother said as she overheard what he had said to Jenny. "There'll be no mysteries if I can help it. I'm not over the scare of those bank robbers last year. Jack," she spoke sternly, "I want you to put all thoughts of robbers and smugglers out of your mind or I might have to pack up and take us all back home on the next flight!"

"Sorry, Mom, but there's nothing wrong with dreaming, is there?" he answered with a disarming smile. "Besides, the best thing that happened last year was the night that Tim and Ruth prayed to receive Jesus into their lives."

"And wouldn't it be great if Mr. and Mrs. Chen accepted the Lord this year?" chimed in Jenny.

"Now that's something we all can agree on," Dad said as he patted his wife's hand. "And, we'll just leave the robbers in God's hands. That's the safest thing to do."

For several months, Jack and Jenny had been begging for another trip to Hong Kong while Tim and Ruth had done their share of pleading with their dad.

"It all depends on Mr. Carlton's business," he kept reminding them.

Several weeks passed before the phone rang in Mr. Chen's office. "Oh, hello, Mr.

Carlton," he had said as he recognized his friend's voice. "So that means you will be coming out to Hong Kong in June for several weeks?" he exclaimed excitedly. "Just wait until my children hear that! They have been begging me to invite your children for another visit!"

"I would never be able to come alone," he confessed. "Jack and Jenny have been begging for another trip, too. But I hope we can have a quiet three weeks without any incidents with smugglers!"

"Mrs. Chen has remarked several times that she would love to see your family again, but she doesn't want any more experiences with robbers like last year."

"I agree," Mr. Carlton replied. "One episode will last us for a life time."

****

"Just one more hour," Jack said excitedly. "I can hardly wait."

"And remember," replied Jenny, "we have three weeks this time. I'm looking forward to swimming at Repulse Bay and another trip on the cable car to Victoria Peak."

"Ah, that's too mild," Jack grinned. "I want to sail around some of the islands. Maybe there still are some smugglers there that need to be caught!"

"Jack, you have a one track mind, I'd say," Jenny responded with a muffled laugh. "But don't let Mom hear that, or you'll be on the next plane back!"

Collecting their baggage as quickly as possible, they headed toward the Customs inspector who cleared them in a few minutes. Rushing ahead of their parents, they burst out into the waiting area for a noisy reunion with their two friends. The trip to the Repulse Bay apartment brought back a lot of memories. If anyone could have read the boys' minds at that moment, they would have been shocked at the thoughts of robbers and smugglers dancing around in their heads. It was going to be an exciting summer if the boys had anything to do about it!

Chapter 2

The Perfect Crime

When are we going to visit the floating restaurant again?" the four kids kept asking. "Remember, that's where Jack found the Orient jewel in the pouch as we were leaving the restaurant," Jenny reminded her parents.

"We remember all right," replied Mother, "only this time, we're not going back there. The memory is still too vivid and scary for me." And then, looking at her children she added, "And I hope for you two also!"

"No way," Jack spoke up with excitement. "I'm not looking for robbers, but I would like some excitement."

"I'd much rather think about the spiritual growth in Tim and Ruth," replied Mother.

"Pastor Whitehead's last letter said that the children and Mrs. Chen haven't missed a Sunday since we were here. Mr. Chen attended only once at Christmas time to see his children in the Christmas program."

"We just need to continue praying for them," replied Dad. "God will do the rest."

"Tim thinks his mother really believes," added Jack, "but she's afraid Mr. Chen would object. He's very much opposed to any of them being Christians, but I don't understand why anyone would object," he said with a puzzled frown on his face.

"Jack, Chinese people have been Buddhists for many centuries," Mother replied. "All their ancestors have been Buddhists. Many Chinese people think that Christianity is for Americans, and Buddhism is for the Chinese."

"You see, Jack," added Dad, "they don't understand that salvation and eternal life is for everyone and that it only comes through

Jesus Christ. That's why we must continue to pray for them every day."

Later that day, in a quiet corner at their apartment swimming pool, the four friends talked about that very subject. Jack led them in prayer. "Lord Jesus, we pray that Tim and Ruth's parents will soon understand the way of salvation. Help us to be good witnesses to them. In Jesus' name, Amen."

"Thanks, Jack," Tim responded quietly. "It's really neat to have friends who pray for our parents and us."

Jack nodded in agreement, and then, he remembered some important news he had to share. "Next week our family will be going to a resort hotel in the New Territories across from Lantau Island. Dad said you could come out every day on the train and, best of all, he said your folks had agreed to the plan."

"Really?" exclaimed Ruth as she clapped her hands. "There are a lot of places out there for us to explore. It's not as crowded as it is here in town."

"That's right, Jack," responded Tim with enthusiasm, "and there's an old temple there, too. It's kind of a spooky place."

Ruth nodded in agreement. "There's not much light in the buildings either, except the little that comes in through some small windows near the ceiling. And, there are many rooms filled with big scary-looking statues of old Chinese gods."

"And she means scary," Tim exclaimed with a shudder. "The whole place is dark and musty. You know what? I can think of a dozen places there that would be a perfect place to hide stolen loot!"

"Boy that sounds like fun! Are you girls going exploring with us?" asked Jack.

"We sure are!" they exclaimed in unison. "You couldn't possibly leave us at the hotel!"

"But don't breathe a word to Mom," cautioned Jenny. "She's so concerned that something dangerous will happen to us again this summer."

"My mom feels that way, too," said Tim, "but we keep telling her that no matter what happens, the Lord will take care of us. Ruth and I have learned a lot about the Bible at our church. Pastor Whitehead said that very thing last Sunday in his sermon."

"Oh, Jack and Jenny, wouldn't it have been awful if you hadn't come to Hong Kong last summer? We never would have met you, and we would never have heard about Jesus and how to get to heaven."

****

Later that night, Mr. Carlton heard a report on the late evening news.

"An armored bank truck was hijacked at an isolated spot on a highway in the New

Territories," the reporter announced. "A couple of farmers working in their field reported a car pulled out in front of the armored vehicle, and then two others suddenly came in behind."

Mr. Carlton sat transfixed as he watched the TV news. Some farmers had watched it happen. "The first car forced the truck to stop by blocking the road, and then suddenly, the back door of the truck swung open, and the men inside began tossing bags of money out to the men from the cars. Everyone was furiously scrambling around to get the money transferred to the car. In just a few minutes, it was all over," added the farmers.

"Two hours later, the empty truck was discovered on an isolated back road. The driver and helper were both missing. No trace of the robbers has been found," continued the newscaster. "Everything in the truck is missing and there are no signs of the getaway cars. There are no clues either!"

Mrs. Carlton gasped as she put down her needlepoint and listened intently.

"The police are inspecting the truck very carefully," the reporter continued, "as they search for finger prints. Thus far, they have not found any. The only lead they have so far is the fact that the helper on the armored car is a newly-hired security guard who has been on the job less than six weeks. The police believe, at this point, that this is an inside job," continued the reporter with this startling news. "In fact, at this point, it looks like the perfect crime."

"Oh, don't tell me there's another big robbery!" she said with a heavy sigh. "Oh, Lord, take care of us and keep us out of this mess!"

"We can't possibly be involved in anything as serious as this a second time," Mr. Carlton said reassuringly. "That would just be too unusual."

But he wondered to himself about his inquisitive children. *If there is a mystery to be solved, they always seem to get involved somehow,* he thought.

Turning to his wife, he said, "The Hong Kong police are the best in the world. Hopefully, they'll have those robbers in jail by morning!"

"I would like to think that would happen," she replied with a tinge of anxiety in her voice, "but this looks like a perfect, well-planned inside job. I'm afraid it's going to take longer than that. Please don't breathe a word to the children! That's all we need to spoil our vacation!"

Chapter 3

A Trip to the New Territories

"Okay, everyone," announced Dad to his excited children at the breakfast table, "we'll shove off by ten o'clock for a beautiful quiet hotel in the New Territories. This is going to be a fun-filled week for all of us with swimming and visits to some interesting tourist sights of the area."

He had listened to the early morning newscast, but he didn't mention one word about yesterday's robbery. The news report said there was no sign of the robbers or the two men supposedly taken captive. "The police are theorizing," the announcer had stated, "that at least one of the guards was working with the robbers since the whole operation had taken place so quickly and without a struggle."

As the car pulled away from their home, Jack asked, "How long will the trip be to the hotel?"

"About an hour," Dad replied as he adjusted the radio dial to some soft music.

"Oh, look at that farmer working in the fields with his water buffalo," Jenny exclaimed in surprise. "The plow he's using is so old-fashioned!"

"That sure seems like hard work," Jack added as he turned to see as much as he could. "See that boy carrying a load on his shoulder pole! I bet he's my age!"

"Children do a lot of hard work in farm families everywhere," Mother said, "but these children seem to have extra heavy burdens."

"There's a temple way up on that hill over there," Jack said pointing to the right. "Tim was telling us there is an old temple near our hotel with lots of places to explore. He has been there several times and says it is really a neat place. There are some very old, scary-looking idols in the big temple. He said they are several hundred years old. Can you imagine people worshipping at a place like that?"

"You know, Jack," replied Dad, "the Chinese people don't know of anything better than their old gods. That's why we send missionaries to tell them of the true God and salvation in Jesus Christ."

"I guess that's right," Jack acknowledged. "Tim says the people are always afraid of these gods and don't have any feelings of love as we do for Jesus."

"That is the great difference between Christianity and all other religions. We have a personal relationship with Jesus and that makes all the difference in the world."

A few minutes later, Jenny said, "Dad, I'm so glad you invited Tim and Ruth to come out tomorrow. I wouldn't want to be in Hong Kong and not be able to see them every day."

"I'm glad they can come. Mrs. Chen said it was not difficult at all for them to come out on the train for a visit," Dad responded. "We just need to get them on their way home by four o'clock. I think it would be nice for Mrs. Chen to come out some time, too."

Unexpectedly, as they were driving along, the music on the radio was interrupted by a special news bulletin. Before Dad realized what was happening, the announcer was already into the bulletin.

"Yesterday's armored truck robbery in the New Territories is still a big mystery," he was saying.

Suddenly, the car became deathly quiet as Jack and Jenny strained to hear every word. It was too late now. The news was out and the twins were sitting on the edge of their seats listening intently.

"The robbers and the money have all disappeared, and there is no sign of them anywhere," the announcer continued. "Several road blocks have been set up in an attempt to intercept the robbers, but nothing suspicious has been reported so far. None of the witnesses got any license numbers as they were out in their fields working. The only clue the police have is that the lead car was a long, sleek, gray European-made car. All the windows were tinted and there are no clues about what the men look like or how many were involved. They estimated there were at least six people involved. That is all the news for now. Stay tuned to this station for further updates on the hour." The announcer signed off and the music resumed.

"Dad, what's that all about?" exploded Jack in surprise. "When did it happen? Did you know about it?"

"We heard the first reports late last night after you all went to bed," Dad replied, "and because we were coming out to the New Territories today, we didn't want either of you to become worried. Last night the police were hoping to have the robbers in jail by this morning."

"Boy, this sounds exciting! I wonder if Captain Ling is still in charge at the police department. I wonder if he will be involved in this case," Jack exclaimed with excitement. "Tim said the New Territories is a very large area with lots of people living there. I bet it's going to be hard to locate those robbers."

As Dad was explaining all he had heard last night and early this morning, the traffic slowed to a crawl and then stopped. They inched along every few seconds until Dad could see the police officers ahead.

"This is one of the road blocks, I think. There is nothing to worry about though. The police will look into the car for anything suspicious, and they'll just send us on through."

Just as Dad had said, the police looked in and then waved the Americans on.

"Where would the robbers hide all the money?" asked Jenny. "Do you think they would try and cross the border into mainland China? They couldn't carry it all on an airplane."

"You're right, Jenny," responded her dad. "They couldn't possibly take it on a plane, and I doubt that they could cross the border into China with all that money. And besides, I don't think they could make any use of it there. They're probably in hiding and will lay low for a long time. Otherwise, they would be caught immediately."

"That's what robbers do when they pull off a big job like this. They hide out for a long time," said Jack in an authoritative voice. "It looks like they pulled off the perfect crime."

Here we are on our way to the New Territories where the robbery took place, thought Mom fearfully. *There's no telling where the robbers might be. For all I know they might be right in our hotel.* The thought sent shivers up and down her spine as she imagined the worst.

"Please children," she pleaded. "Let's all stay out of this. Let the police handle it. They are trained for such things. I don't want you getting any wild ideas of solving this mystery when the Chens come tomorrow! Do you understand that?"

The twins knew she was upset. "We'll be careful, Mom, and we'll do just as you tell us," they replied.

Dad smiled and Mother looked relieved, but secretly she knew her twins were notorious at sniffing out trouble. Then she remembered how the Lord had watched over them on the last trip, and she was thankful that He was always watching over them.

Chapter 4

An Unexpected Discovery

The next day dawned bright and clear. "Hurry, Jenny, it's almost time for Tim and Ruth to arrive."

"I'm coming," she called trying to catch up with Jack who was already on his way to the train station.

What a day they had! Roaming the beach at the hotel didn't yield any sea shells, but it was fun catching fish and building sand castles.

"Would Tim and Ruth be able to come back tomorrow?" Mr. Carlton asked the Chens that evening when he called to make sure they had arrived home safely.

"We don't want them to be a nuisance to you," Mr. Chen responded.

"Oh, don't worry about that. Jack and Jenny have already informed us that tomorrow would be a very dull day unless your children were here!"

"I know," he responded, "Tim and Ruth feel the same way. Are you sure they will not interfere with your vacation plans?"

"Mr. Chen," he responded with a big chuckle, "by this time you must know that our children just have to be together to have any fun."

"Well, I don't have to ask them if they want to visit you again. Yes, they'll be there at the same time."

"Great! Jack and Jenny will be waiting."

****

"The temple is within walking distance of our hotel, Dad," Jack pleaded. "We won't go anywhere else."

"That's a promise," Tim added.

"Well, okay then. Only to the temple and back."

"Be sure to be back by four o'clock," called Mrs. Carlton. "Remember, Tim and Ruth's train leaves at four-thirty."

"Let's go," called Jack.

"Thanks, Mr. Carlton," Tim called back as the four trooped off to the temple a mile away at the edge of town.

"Look at all the older people trudging along this dirt road to the temple," exclaimed Jenny sympathetically. "They look so tired."

"Some of them have been on the way here for days or even weeks," Tim responded. "Many of them have waited all their lives to make this last trip to the temple. They hope they'll find the way to the life beyond death right here."

"Look at the size of that Buddha," Jack exclaimed in amazement as they entered the main temple building. "It must be 50 or 60 feet high!"

"Not only that," Tim added, "it's covered with gold! That's why it glistens in the rays of the sun coming through that little window up there."

Jack gasped as his eyes became accustomed to the dim light in the building. "Jenny, look at all those little Buddhas lining the four walls, row upon row. There must be hundreds of them! Are these all covered with gold leaf?" he asked in amazement. "They must be worth a fortune."

"You're right about that, Jack," responded Ruth who was also awed by the sight.

"Actually," Tim added, "there are probably a few thousand of those little Buddhas, and they're all covered with gold!"

As they were looking at this amazing sight, an elderly woman approached the altar that was beautifully decorated with flowers and fruit.

"Watch that elderly woman," Tim said in a whisper. "See, she's putting a burning incense stick in that urn. It's supposed to be a prayer to the Buddha. Our Mom does that every day at our family altar in our kitchen. Mom does what that woman is also doing. See, she's clapping her hands to let the Buddha know she's there. Now she'll bow and say a prayer. Mom does the same thing every day. We're praying that, someday, Mom and Dad will come to know Jesus and then really get answers to prayer."

Fascinated, Jack and Jenny stood there in silence. *Imagine praying to an idol,* they thought. *Yes, it has big ears, but they cannot here. It has big eyes, but they cannot see. It has hands, but it cannot reach out and touch the old lady or answer her prayers.* Now they understood a little better what Tim and Ruth had told them when they first met about never getting answers to their prayers.

Jenny whispered to Jack, "Oh, I wish I could speak Chinese and tell her about Jesus."

Jack nodded in agreement. Tim understood how the twins were feeling. "Old Chinese people rarely give up Buddhism for Christianity because they have trusted the idols so long. They would be afraid to change. Our church is full of young people and quite a few older people who became Christians when they were young. That's why Pastor Whitehead emphasizes the importance of working with children and young people. It seems easier to come to Jesus when you are young."

"That's also true in America," said Jack with a nod. "More people accept Jesus when they are young than when they are old. I guess that means we should really work hard to invite all our friends to come to Jesus."

"We've been doing just that," replied Tim. "Quite a few of our classmates are starting to attend church with us. Because you told us about Jesus, now we can tell our friends about Him. You see how hopeless it is for a person to pray to Buddha? The answers never come. That old lady will go away with the same empty feeling in her heart that we used to have," added Tim. "Our parents still have that empty feeling, too. Please pray for them to believe in Jesus."

"We do pray for them every day, and have ever since we met you," Jenny assured him.

"Thanks a lot," replied Ruth as she gave Jenny a big hug. "We believe both of our parents will come to Jesus some day. But it looks like it will take a miracle to get Dad to believe. He seems determined that we should all remain Buddhists."

"Our family will keep praying for them," said Jack. "What's in these other rooms, Tim?" he asked as they entered another room.

"Just more idols and prayer places. On special occasions and religious holidays, this place is packed with people. There are always several places where you can have your fortune told by an old man with a stringy beard or buy incense to burn here," added Tim. "Small idols for your home are also very popular. And, of course, there are lots of places to buy food! Say, talking about food makes me hungry. Let's go over to that little stand to get some Chinese sweet bean cakes. I think you'll like them."

"Sounds good to me," added Jack, as they headed in that direction.

"I'm famished," responded Jenny. "I haven't had anything to eat since breakfast."

"How about some noodles, too?" asked Ruth. "Bean cakes and noodles will make a good meal."

Sitting down on the little wooden stools, Tim ordered the food. "Say, anyone want some octopus?' he asked with a big grin.

"No, thank you!" Jenny replied emphatically.

"What does it taste like?" asked Jack inquisitively.

"Oh, there's not much taste. It reminds me of chewing on a rubber band. Here try a little piece," Tim said laughingly as he brought over the steaming bowls of noodles and a small plate of octopus.

"You sure described it right," Jack acknowledged as he chewed away on a piece. "No taste and just like a rubber band! I think I'll stick to noodles and bean cakes, if you don't mind."

"That's okay," Ruth said with a knowing smile, "it's not my favorite either."

"Boy, these bean cakes are delicious," exclaimed Jack as he reached for a second one. "We'll have to get Mom to buy some."

"I'm full," Jenny said as they headed back to the temple to explore the old buildings out back.

Chapter 4: An Unexpected Discovery

"Look at those old rundown-looking buildings with thatched roofs," Jack exclaimed in surprise.

"Farmers still use a special grass to make roofs like this for their houses and barns," Tim explained as they wandered over to take a better look.

"It looks like a very old building," Jack said as he inspected it more carefully.

Stepping inside the open doorway, they had difficulty seeing at first, because it was so dark.

"Wow! Look at this place," Tim exclaimed as his eyes became accustomed to the dim light. "There sure is a lot of stuff piled all around the walls. And look at that huge pile of rice stalks over there! They must be piled up six or seven feet high!"

"There are no windows in here," Jenny said in surprise. "Do people live in here?"

"I don't think so," said Ruth. "It looks more like a barn to me. See, there are some farm tools over there."

"Hey look over there. That looks like a tire to me!" Jack said in surprise as he peered at it more closely.

"That's a tire all right behind that pile of stalks."

Every eye turned toward the huge pile of rice stalks. When Tim, who was closest to the tire, pulled the stalks aside, he exclaimed, "Hey, look at this! There's a car under this pile of stalks."

As he moved a few stalks aside, he uncovered the fender of a car! Puzzled, they all gathered around to take a look.

Jack let out a low whistle, "Hey, you know what? This could be the missing robbers' car! Remember how one of the cars was gray?" Four pairs of eyes stared at the gray fender.

"Look at the length of this pile?" Jack continued. "I think it's long enough to fit the description of the car the police are looking for!"

They stood there transfixed. Could it possibly be the robbers' car? They felt along the huge pile. Sure enough, there was a car under that pile!

"If this really is the robbers' car, and someone finds us in here—we'll be in for a lot of trouble!" Jack said. "Jenny, take a look out the door and see if anyone is around. We'd better make sure this is the getaway car and then get out of here in a hurry. No telling what would happen to us if we were caught in here!"

Jenny rushed over and peaked out the door.

Ruth said in a hushed voice, "I think we better get out of here while we can. If the robbers return and find us here, we're in real trouble."

"But we need to do a little more investigating," said Tim looking around hurriedly.

"Ruth, you and Jenny stand by the door and watch. If you see anything suspicious, give us a signal. Jack and I need to see if it is a European car or not. Keep a sharp eye on what's happening and let us know if you see anyone coming."

The boys carefully pushed some stalks aside at the other end of the pile of rice stalks. Sure enough it was a European car! No doubt about it. This had to be the robbers' car! What a find!

"We've got to get to the police right away," Jack said as they stood there almost speechless. "They can stake out this place and maybe catch the robbers when they return."

Chapter 5

The Secret Door

The boys were trembling with excitement over their unexpected discovery. They were sure they had stumbled on to the get-a-way car, and they needed to get the news to the police immediately.

"Let's get out of here!" exclaimed Tim.

"But first, we have to rearrange these stalks so the robbers won't know anyone has been here," said Jack with an air of command in his voice. "We don't want the gang to be alerted before the police are ready to make an arrest. I'm sure they will want to get the master-mind behind all of this."

"You're right," agreed Tim as he and Jack began rearranging the stalks around the car.

Tim was up by the front of the car when he noticed a brick in the wall with three holes on the right side. *That's unusual,* he thought. *Why would one brick have three holes on one side just as if they were made for three fingers?* Without thinking, he instinctively inserted three fingers into the holes and gently wiggled the brick. It began to move! It slid out about 5 inches and stopped! Suddenly, there was a soft grinding sound that startled everyone. Some of the stalks appeared to be moving, too!

"What was that?" asked Ruth as she moved to Jenny's side.

"I don't know," replied Tim. "I pulled on this brick with the three holes on its side, and it slid out a few inches. Then the noise started. It sounds like a motor is working."

Jack pulled more stalks aside, and to everyone's amazement, they saw a narrow doorway about two feet wide.

Chapter 5: The Secret Door

Jack was the first to recover from the surprise. "Tim, this must be a secret door!" he said. "That brick triggered the latch and opened the door. I bet those robbers have stashed the money inside somewhere. Boy, wouldn't it be something if we found the money here?"

"Wow, that would be something!" whistled Tim. "But we'd better hurry and find out, so we can get out of here before we get caught."

"You're right," replied Jack with tension filling his voice. "You girls keep a watch. I have a little flash light. Tim and I will just take a look inside the door. Maybe the money will be there."

"Okay, but you guys better hurry up," pleaded Ruth. "I'm scared."

"We'll just take a peek," Jack replied as he started through the narrow doorway.

The girls took up their positions at the door and kept an eye on all that was going on outside while the boys carefully slid through the narrow opening. Jack's flashlight didn't reach very far in the blackness of the room. *How big is this place? Where does it lead? Is the money in here?* A hundred thoughts crowded his mind.

"Boy, its dark in here," Tim said in a hushed voice. "And scary, too."

"I hope there are no snakes in here," Jack said as he played the little flash light around the large empty room. "This light is so small. I can't see anything that looks like money bags."

"You know what I think?" Tim said. "I think we're right under that big Buddha in the temple. I've heard stories that long ago robbers sometimes hid treasure inside the Buddha for safe keeping. People would never suspect money or jewels to be hidden inside because they would be afraid to come near the idol. It gave thieves a natural hiding place."

"Really?" exclaimed Jack in surprise. "But, of course! That makes sense! It would be a natural hiding place for treasure. I sure wish I had a bigger flashlight. This one's not much good in such a big place."

As the boys crept forward cautiously, they realized they had to keep that little slit of light from the doorway in sight, or they might get lost in the darkness. With their hearts beating wildly, they moved forward very slowly. Tim clung to Jack's shirt to keep them from getting separated in the darkness. Just then, Jack stumbled on something! He stopped and lowered the light for a closer look. Tim bent forward to get a better look, too.

"It's a bag," Jack whispered loudly. "And look! Here are some Chinese characters on the bag! What does it say, Tim?"

"Let me see," he said as he bent over to get a look at the characters in the dim light. "Jack! This is one of the money bags! This is the name of the bank! We've found the money, Jack! This is where they've hidden the money."

As Jack moved the light around, they realized they had bumped into a huge pile of money bags.

"This is it, all right," agreed Jack excitedly. "We've found the money!"

"Now, let's get out of here quick," said Tim. "No telling when those robbers will return. We would be in big trouble if they caught us in here."

"Right! Let's get going," Jack said as he turned toward the little bit of light coming from the doorway. The boys had just squeezed out of the doorway and were arranging the stalks when the girls came rushing over whispering excitedly.

"A car with four men just pulled in at the far end of the court! They're headed right this way!" Panic gripped all four of them as they tried to figure out what to do next.

Chapter 5: The Secret Door

"Quick! Crawl in here at the front end of the car," ordered Tim as he pulled some stalks aside. "There's enough room for the four of us, I think. Just be careful not to pull the stalks aside and uncover the open door to the secret room. We'll be safe here if we don't make a sound."

He pushed the girls in first as he told them hurriedly about finding the money bags. Then he and Jack crawled in.

"It's dusty smelling back here," Jenny whispered. "I hope we won't be in here too long!"

As Jack arranged the stalks to cover their hiding place, he whispered, "Everyone okay? Enough room?"

"Okay," they all whispered.

"But it's hot in here! Not too much air either," whispered Jenny who was wedged in the back.

"Shhhhhhh!" Jack whispered.

It was cramped for the four of them, and the warm sunny day made it even hotter. *How long will we have to hide here?* Jack wondered. Just then they heard the men enter the barn and pull the doors shut behind them.

"Who left this door open?" one of the men growled. "Who was out last? If anybody was snooping around, we'll be in trouble with the boss."

They were talking in muffled voices and in Chinese, so only Tim and Ruth could understand what they were saying.

"One of those guys is angry that the door was left open," Tim whispered. "They're talking about the robbery! One of them said they were lucky no one was snooping around."

"What are they saying now?" Jack whispered.

"They're laughing about pulling off the robbery," Tim said, "and bragging about how clever they were and how mystified the police are at the disappearance of the two men on the truck." He paused, and continued, "Those fellows were part of the gang! That's why it was so easy to pull it off."

An hour passed as the men discussed many details of the robbery and the money hidden in the secret room under the Buddha. Tim whispered the translation of their conversation for Jack and Jenny.

"No one even knows about the secret room," one of the men boasted. "It's been a secret in our family for many years. Some old priest built it as a hiding place from thieves and bandits who used to roam this part of the country."

Tim paused, and listened. Picking up the story, he continued translating. "My uncle's father," said the man, "was a priest in those days and told my father about it. The boss was real happy when I told him about this place. He even said he would give me a bigger cut of the money for this information when he divides it up."

As the four kids huddled in the darkness, they wondered, *Will we ever get out of here alive? We have a lot of valuable information to give to the police.* It was hot and stuffy, and the straw made them feel itchy all over. *How much longer will we have to hide here?* Each wondered.

Jack looked at his watch. He could hardly make out the time. *Four thirty! That's a half hour after we were supposed to be back home!* "Better pray that they leave soon," he whispered. "We're a half hour late getting home."

"Keep it low, Jack," whispered Tim. "These are desperadoes for sure."

The stifling air and the dust from the rice stalks were beginning to affect Jenny. *What can I do? I feel like I'm going to sneeze!* Panic seized her! She clamped her hand over her mouth to muffle the sneeze, but it was too late! “Ka-choo!” The sound of her sneeze seemed to echo throughout the whole barn!

Chapter 6

Caught!

Everyone froze. They waited in petrified silence. They didn't have long to wait. The startled robbers jumped up from the table.

"What was that?" one exclaimed. "Sounded like somebody sneezed."

Frantically they began looking all around the room. It was clear by the sound of their voices they were very upset and angry. The children didn't move a muscle. Frightened because they were discovered, each was praying for God to protect them. The robbers were looking everywhere. Then someone moved closer to the rice stalks. One of the robbers was reaching among the stalks.

He touched Jack's arm! He yelled, pulled the stalks away and jerked Jack out!

Jack stood there with four pair of eyes glaring at him. The men talked excitedly in Chinese, and then one of the men pulled the stalks aside to see if anyone else was hiding in there. Tim was the next one pulled out and then the two girls. Jenny was crying softly, knowing her sneeze had given them away. She stood there dejected and frightened. Seeing the two Chinese kids, the men directed their questions to them in Chinese.

"What are you kids doing in here?" they demanded. "Where did you come from? Don't you know this is private property?"

Tim did his best to answer the barrage of questions that were being fired at him. The other three prayed for the Lord's help. The four men were talking fast and furiously now. One of them, who seemed to be the leader, exclaimed angrily, "They must have overheard everything we've been talking about! Two of these kids are Chinese, so they understand everything!"

"If it was just these foreigners, it wouldn't be too bad," he continued, "but these Chinese kids are a real problem. We've got a big problem on our hands!"

One of the men directed a question at Jack and Jenny in broken English. "You understand Chinese? What you do here?" he demanded.

They shook their heads, "No." Fear gripped their hearts as they realized their dangerous predicament.

"Honest," Jack responded with quivering voice. "We only know a few Chinese words. Please let us go."

"But your friends. They understand," sneered the robber as he glanced at Tim and Ruth with a sinister grin.

No matter how they pleaded to be let go, it did no good. They had heard too much, and now they had seen the robbers' faces as well.

One of the men, with a ruthless grimace on his face, spoke to one of the other men. “Go call the boss and tell him what happened. These kids must be disposed of----and quick!”

Those were ominous words. The four huddled close together for comfort, and Ruth began to cry with Jenny, as they held hands. *It was all my fault. If I hadn’t sneezed, we would never have been discovered,* Jenny thought. *Too late now! Oh Lord, we’re in a big mess, and it’s all my fault,* she cried inwardly as the leader pushed them into a corner and repeated his order to call the boss and report what had happened.

“No way I’m going to call him,” exclaimed the man, obviously frightened. “I’m not taking the rap for this. You’re in charge. You call him.”

“You heard me,” retorted the leader angrily. “Now get going! It’s the guy who left the door open who is in trouble. The boss will settle that later, but go and get his instructions---now!"

The man left, returning in a few minutes to report in a trembling voice. "Two men are to bring the kids to the Twin Dragon, and the other two are to fix up the hiding place again--- and this time, lock the door! The boss is furious with all of us, and he said we would all be punished for our carelessness." They looked fearfully at each other, and then glared at the kids who had gotten them into this mess. "Okay, get them in the car," the leader ordered, "and you two," pointing to two of the men, "get this place fixed up securely again."

****

Meanwhile, back at the Carltons, Mrs. Carlton was anxiously watching the clock. It was four-thirty! *Jack and Jenny always report in if they are going to be late,* she thought.

They're a half hour late and no sign or word from them. Oh, what could have happened to them? she thought.

"Maybe we should walk over to the temple and see if anything is wrong. I'm worried," she said to her husband.

"That's a good idea, but maybe you should stay here," he said, obviously concerned, too. "Someone should be here in case they telephone. Now don't worry. They are all responsible children. We must trust the Lord to care for them wherever they are."

At the temple, Mr. Carlton stopped and asked a shopkeeper, "Have you seen any sign of four children—two Chinese and two Americans?"

"I don't remember seeing four children," the man replied. He turned and asked some other people nearby. "No one remembers seeing them," he replied.

Walking slowly around the temple area, he searched everywhere, and then proceeded to the barn where the children were being held. There was no sign of them anywhere.

****

Inside the barn, the robbers were hustling the trembling children into the back seat of a car. As it backed out of the barn and pulled swiftly away, they saw Mr. Carlton! Spontaneously, they all yelled to get his attention. One of the men turned around and shouted for them to be quiet or he would beat them into silence. The windows were tinted a very dark color, so it was impossible for Mr. Carlton to see them.

Chapter 7

The Search

The car made its way through the crowded streets and on through the harbor tunnel out to a small marina on Hong Kong island. Jack looked at his watch. "Almost six o'clock," he whispered as he pointed to his watch. "Our folks are going to be very worried!"

The man in the front seat turned around and slapped Jack. "Didn't I tell you not to talk?" he snarled. "If you don't do as you're told, we'll teach you a lesson. We're in a heap of trouble already because of you kids. It would be a pleasure to punish you for your snooping around our barn!"

Shudders ran up and down their spines at the threatening tone in his voice, and they dared not talk to each other again, but each one was praying desperately for God's miraculous intervention.

Back at the hotel, the worried parents had called the Chens and told them of the children's disappearance. Hearing the frightening news, the Chens were equally upset and anxious for the safety of their children.

"Mr. Carlton, call the local police station right away. They can all speak English. We'll be at your place in about an hour," Mr. Chen said.

"I've already called them, and they assured me they would put out an immediate alert," replied Mr. Carlton.

****

In a few minutes, the police were knocking on their hotel door. The officers listened attentively, getting the descriptions of the children and how they were dressed. Later, when the police questioned the people in and around the temple, no one remembered seeing the four children. They found no clues. They were at a dead-end, but they assured the anxious parents that a very careful search would continue to be made. When the Chens arrived, the anxious parents sat together--- worried and wondering. Mr. Carlton finally broke the awful silence and suggested they pray for the children's safety.

When he finished, Mrs. Chen said, "Oh, thank you Mr. Carlton. All this year my children have been telling me how Jesus answers their prayers. Praying with us makes me feel much better. I have listened to Pastor Whitehead when I take the children to church. He always has something very helpful to tell us. I'm not a Christian, although I do believe that Jesus is a wonderful friend and helper. Tim and Ruth are always telling us how good it is to be a Christian."

"That's right," said Mr. Chen. "I guess I'm the one who has been holding everyone back. You see, my family has always been Buddhists and in our Chinese religion, the eldest son must carry on the family tradition of praying for the ancestors. My elderly mother is very concerned about our children attending the Christian church. She keeps saying, 'Who is going to pray for you when you are dead? Son, don't forsake me. You must pray for me when I am dead. And, don't forget your father. He has been dead for several years now. Son, he is counting on you to pray for him.'"

"But I see how my children are so happy and changed. I always thought Christianity was for westerners and not for Chinese. Now I am not so sure anymore. Still, I cannot forsake my elderly parents."

Worried as they were about the children, the Carltons were joyful at these words from Mr. Chen. They knew Mrs. Chen was very close to becoming a Christian, but were surprised Mr. Chen was so honest about his spiritual condition.

"You are being very honest about a very difficult situation you're facing, Mr. Chen," replied Mr. Carlton, "but let me share with you an important truth from the Bible. While we are alive, each person must make a personal decision to follow Jesus who alone can give eternal life. I understand your concern for your parents, and the Chinese custom of praying for their ancestors. Nevertheless, the Bible teaches us that the most important thing any of us can do is to come to Jesus ourselves and ask Him into our lives as our Savior. Then He can help us. In addition, He promised to give us wisdom in every situation we face."

The four fell into a long period of silence, each with their own thoughts. Suddenly the eerie silence was broken by the ringing of the telephone. Mr. Carlton picked it up quickly, hoping it was the police with news of the children. To his surprise, he heard the familiar voice of Captain Ling.

"Mr. Carlton," he said, "I'm very sorry to hear about the disappearance of your children. I assure you that we will do everything we can to locate them and return them to you and the Chens safely. Just sit tight. The police there have assured me they're doing everything possible to locate them. I'll get back to you as soon as I have any word."

"Thank you, Captain," replied Mr. Carlton. "I didn't expect we would be involved in another crisis in Hong Kong. Yes, I know they are four resourceful children. We have prayed for their safety, and I believe God will protect them and help you locate them."

"We'll do our best to make it quick, Mr. Carlton. Greetings to everyone there. And by the way, since you were last here, you might like to know that my wife and I have gone back to church, and we can join you in praying for the children."

"That's wonderful news, Captain. That certainly encourages all of us."

When he hung up, Mr. Carlton repeated all that Captain Ling had told him and the Carltons rejoiced at another answer to prayer.

Chapter 8

Attempted Escape

In the car, the children stared anxiously at each other as many thoughts raced through their minds. *Who was going to save them now? How would they ever escape from these ruthless men?*

When the car stopped, the leader got out and told the driver to watch the kids. Then he walked briskly toward a small boat tied up at the pier and spoke with a man in the boat.

Jack knew they were in a desperate situation and time was running out. He was wracking his brain for a way of escape, but every idea seemed impossible. He stretched his legs out, and his foot touched something. It was a large wine bottle! Suddenly, a plan formed in his mind. *There's only one man in the car,* he thought, *and he's in the front seat. If somehow we could distract him, maybe, just maybe, I could get the bottle and knock him out.* It was worth a chance.

He poked Tim and whispered nervously, "Lunge toward the other side of the car when I give you a poke and attempt to open the door. I've found a bottle here, and I think I can knock this guy out!"

Tim nodded in agreement, but he wondered, *Will this plan work?* He was fearful.

Jack spoke up sharply in a loud voice that startled everyone in the car, including the driver who turned toward Jack and shouted, "Shut up! And, don't move!"

Jack shouted again and pointed out the window of the car. "Look who's coming over there!"

The driver turned to look, and when he did, Jack gave Tim a poke. Tim reacted immediately and lunged toward the side of the car. The startled driver turned back toward Tim and shouted for him to sit down. Tim managed to open the door just as Jack swung the bottle at the driver's head, knocking him out. Tim pushed the startled girls out of the car. "Run into the bushes," he shouted, "and get as far away from the car as you can!"

All four kids scrambled out and ran for the bushes. They knew they didn't have much time. In the dark they fought their way through the underbrush, stumbling on roots and getting snagged on branches. Hearing the commotion, the first man came running back, shouting for the man in the boat to help. When they reached the car, the kids were nowhere to be seen, and the driver was unconscious. Grabbing a flash light, they played it all over the area. There was no sign of the kids.

"They can't be far from here," he shouted to his companion. "Find them or our goose is cooked!" Both men ran back and forth shining the light in all directions.

Crouching low, the four youngsters huddled together. The men were frantically shouting directions to one another. Then the flashlight played over the area again. It was a powerful light, and they knew they could not go any further. Clinging to each other, they waited breathlessly and wondered what would happen to them.

The driver soon recovered, and rubbing the bump on his head, groggily took up the search with the other two while he listened to them cursing and scolding him for being so careless.

"Quit blaming me," he complained, "You're in charge. Why didn't you tie them up in the first place?"

"Shut up and find those kids or you won't live to see another day," the leader angrily shouted back.

The four kids clung together listening to the angry voices that were coming closer and closer until they could have reached out and touched them. Their hearts were pounding furiously.

Oh, how I wish I could understand Chinese, Jack thought in frustration. He wanted to ask Tim what the men were shouting to each other, but they were too close. No one even dared to whisper a word. *I'll just have to wait and find out later,* he thought. The children breathed a little easier as the men moved on.

"We'll never find them in the dark. Lee, go get the dogs!" the leader commanded. "We'll sniff them out. We can't let them get away!"

As the men moved on, Jack whispered softly, "What was that all about, Tim?"

"Those men are really worried that we escaped. They are blaming one another, and they are afraid of what their boss will do when they meet him," answered Tim solemnly. "The boss must be a terrible man. Now they're going to get some dogs!"

"Oh, no," wailed Jenny softly. "I bet they are ferocious watch dogs! Oh, what are we going to do?"

Lee hurried to get the two dogs locked in a nearby boathouse. The dogs were already howling ferociously at all the noise and commotion and were ready for action. "Okay, guys, I'm coming to let you out. You better find those kids for us or we're in big trouble."

They bounded out the moment the door was opened. The sound of their barking sent shivers up and down the children's spines as they moved slowly, stealthily, hoping to put more distance between themselves and the robbers, but their progress was slow in the dark.

Lee returned with the two dogs straining on their leashes. "Let them loose," shouted the first man. "See if they can pick up the trail of those pesky kids."

The dogs had been yelping and tugging at the leashes, pulling Lee along as they sniffed the area. But now unleashed, they bounded off in the darkness. The kids huddled together again and prayed for God to protect them and throw the dogs off their trail. The dogs bounded ahead at breakneck speed with the angry men following as fast as they could. As the yelping got fainter, the children decided it was time to move again.

"The Lord is answering our prayers. The dogs are going in the opposite direction!" Jack exclaimed excitedly.

Suddenly, there was extra loud shouting from the men and yelping from the dogs. "Here they are!" shouted a man in the distance.

"Don't try and run," someone was shouting, "or the dogs will tear you to pieces!"

The kids shuddered with fear, but Jack realized the dogs had discovered someone else. "They probably discovered a beggar sleeping in the bushes," he said. "This is our chance to get away from here, but we don't have much time. Let's go!"

Jenny had been trying to look around and see if there were any places where they could hide. "Wait a minute, Jack. Look over there. Isn't that a small building? Maybe we could get inside and hide from those dogs."

"Wow, Jenny, you're right. I hadn't seen that before. It's only about fifty yards away. I think we could make it easily."

"Anything would be better than just hiding here in the open," Tim added.

"If we stay here," said Ruth, "the dogs will get us."

"You're right," said Jack. "I think we should try and reach it."

"But they'll see us," objected Tim, obviously very shaken.

"We'll have to take that chance," replied Jack. "Look! The lights are moving away from us now. Let's make a run for it! Be as quiet as possible. Get in the shadow of the building, and let's hope there's a door that's unlocked."

"Okay," they all agreed. Leaving the safety of the bushes, they headed for the shack as quickly and as quietly as possible.

"Sure glad the moon isn't out yet," Tim grunted as he tried to help Ruth.

Suddenly, Jenny stumbled on a big root and letting out a low scream, she fell headlong to the ground.

"Oh, Jenny, be quiet," Jack said softly as he helped her to her feet. "Are you all right?"

"Ouch! I don't think I can make it," she said as she stumbled forward.

"Yes you can." Jack encouraged. "You've got to!" Breathless, they reached the back of the shack without being seen.

"Now, what?" asked Jenny as she sat limply, rubbing her ankle. "Boy! This is scary! Let's get inside. I can't run far on this ankle!"

"I hope it's just sprained," Jack said sympathetically. "If there's an open door or window in this shack, I think we'll be okay. Follow me. There must be a door somewhere."

Jack led the way silently around to the front of the shack and tried opening the door. He turned the knob and pushed gently, hoping there would be no noise.

"Tim, help me push on this door. Maybe it's just stuck." Suddenly the door opened under the weight of the two boys. "Get inside," he ordered the girls who didn't need any urging!

"Lock the door!" whispered Ruth.

In the darkness, the boys were feeling for a bolt. *Was there one on this door?* "Here it is," whispered Jack as he slid the old bolt in place. "Quick, pile everything you can against the door. That will help barricade it and give us extra protection."

"There, that ought to do it," Tim said as he shoved some boxes against the door.

"Those dogs sound terrible," Ruth said with a trembling voice. "At least the dogs can't pounce on us now and tear us to pieces."

"It's a miracle we haven't been caught," said Jack. "Let's take a moment to thank the Lord."

They all bowed their heads as Jack prayed and thanked the Lord for the protection of this old shack.

"But we're not out of trouble yet, Lord," he prayed. "Please show us what to do next." There was a chorus of low "amens" as he finished.

Although they were exhausted from the long ordeal, there was no thought of sleeping. "I sure wish I was home in my bed," Ruth whispered. "I bet there are bugs in this place, too!"

Chapter 9

Discovered

The three frenzied men were flailing the bushes and causing a lot of commotion. "Find those kids or we'll never live to see another day," the leader called to his men. "You know what happened to that stupid guy, Fu, who messed things up. He just disappeared, and we never heard from him again! Find those kids or face the music!" he growled.

By this time, two other men from the gang joined the search. "Follow the dogs," the leader commanded. "They'll find them eventually even though they don't have a scent to follow. Just stay with them and listen for any sounds of those kids in the bushes."

“They can’t be far from here,” shouted one of the men. “There aren’t many places to hide. Keep looking!”

The sounds of the men came closer. There was one small window in the shack which let in a little light from the street light nearby.

“Flatten yourselves against the wall!” Jack ordered. “Someone might shine their search-light through that little window. If you can find anything, cover yourself with it.”

The sounds of the men were coming clos-er and closer again. Now they were circling the shack! They even tried the door!

“Can’t be in there,” one of the men said. “The door is locked.”

“Yeah, but they’ve got to be somewhere around here,” another replied as they moved on. Inside the shack everyone held their breath.

“Boy, that was a close one!” whispered Tim as they heard the men’s footsteps fading away, “Do you think they will come back?”

"I don't know," responded Jack softly, "but just lay low."

The noise continued all around them as the men searched the area. Now the sounds were coming closer again!

"It looks like we lost them," said one man. "Boy, the boss is going to be tough on you guys when he hears about this."

"Hey, shut up and keep looking!" said the leader.

"Okay, okay, but you know it's the truth," the other said.

Now they were standing right outside the shack! The man with the flash light was shining it around when he caught sight of the small window in its light. The kids crouched lower as the rays of light played on the ceiling. The window intrigued the man. *Could the kids be inside?* he wondered.

"Hey, Lee, come over here and give me a boost," he called. "I want to take a look inside this shack, but the window is too high for me."

"The door's locked," objected Lee. "You're just wasting your time."

"Oh, yeah?" replied the man with a nasty sound in his voice. "You can't be too sure. I just got this funny feeling that those kids aren't far from this spot. Now give me a boost and stop complaining."

Lee came over and boosted the man on his shoulders. "Don't take too long," he gasped, "you're heavy!"

As the light played again on the ceiling, the four froze in place, not daring even to breathe.

"Hurry up," called Lee, "I can't hold you up much longer!"

With that, there was a crash and a lot of shouting as Lee fell to his knees, and the man on his shoulders tumbled to the ground.

Cursing Lee, he shouted, "You idiot! What's the matter with you? Are you a weakling?"

The two men were exchanging nasty remarks and blaming each other.

"Get someone to help you," shouted the first man. "Those kids could be inside, and if we don't find them, we're going to suffer for it."

"Okay, okay, but you're heavy," complained Lee.

He shouted for another man to help. The children held their breath and hugged the wall on the side of the room with the window, hoping they wouldn't be discovered. Finally, two men boosted the first man up again and held him steady. He played the light around as he muttered, "Don't see anyone in there."

The four didn't dare move. Then the light came closer. He was shining it straight down the side of the window.

Suddenly, he shouted. “They’re here! They’re here! We’ve found them!”

The other men rushed up to the shack and began pounding on the door. “Open up,” they shouted.

The dogs were yelping madly as the men pounded on the door. No one inside moved. *Couldn’t anyone hear the commotion? Would anyone come to find out what all the shouting was about? Where was God right now?* All kinds of questions were running through their minds. As the pounding increased, the youngsters’ hearts were beating faster and faster. The shack was shaking so much, it seemed the men would push it over!

“Quick. Get that crow bar from the boat,” someone shouted. “We’ll break the door down.”

As the men continued pounding the door, one of them ran back and got the crow bar.

"Gimme that bar," shouted the first man. "You guys watch what you're doing. Don't let them escape."

He began prying on the old hinges of the door. The dried wood splintered and large pieces broke off. The kids knew they were trapped, and this time there was no escape. Finally, with one strong blow, the last rusty old hinge broke loose, and they pulled the door out and let it fall to the ground. A couple of men stumbled over the boxes piled up inside! Each grabbed two kids roughly by the arm as they shouted, "Okay, you kids. Stand up against that wall. We've got you trapped this time, and you won't escape again."

Calling to the other men, they shouted, "We've got them all! They're here in this shack. Come and help us!"

The children were pulled outside, and each was held firmly by one of the gang. Frightened and trembling, they knew they were in trouble. These snarling men were very angry.

"You kids ought to be thrashed good," the first man shouted. "I told you not to try any monkey business with us. Now you're in for it, for sure. I'm gonna tell the boss to put an end to you all. Okay, move them out to the boat. Let's get them on board before something else happens!"

They shoved the kids forward toward the boat. As Jenny stumbled forward, she was thankful the throbbing in her ankle had eased up. The pain was not so bad now. She just hoped nothing more would happen to make the men angrier. As they scrambled into the boat, the engine started, and they lurched forward in the direction of the Twin Dragon.

Chapter 10

A Night on the Twin Dragon

In a few minutes they pulled alongside the large and luxurious Twin Dragon. The four children were hustled up the gangway and into a brightly lit room where a burly-looking man was seated in a big arm chair with two large body guards standing on either side of him. They knew instantly he was the boss! They trembled at the sight of his ugly, snarling face and wondered what he had in store for them.

"So you went snooping around my barn, did you?" he sneered. "Don't you know you should stay out of other people's property? My men tell me you were hiding in the barn behind the rice stalks covering my car. If there are any scratches on it, your folks will pay dearly."

Without pausing, he continued his harangue. "So, you know my car is hidden under the rice stalks? And you heard my men talking together about the robbery, I suppose?" He never gave them a chance to answer.

Then he looked at the two men who brought the children in. "You stupid idiots! Why did you go away and leave the barn door open? Didn't I warn you to be careful? You'll be punished for that, but I'll take care of that later," he snarled angrily as he glared at them coldly. "Now, take these kids to cabin 3 and get Ching to stand guard over them. Tie them up to the chairs yourselves. If they escape--well, you know what will happen to you! Now get out of here. We'll cast off as soon as the tide rises, and then we'll take care of these pesky kids."

Chapter 10: A Night on the Twin Dragon

The four kids were pushed down the passageway by the two men and thrust into Cabin 3. The men immediately began tying each of them securely in a chair.

"Ouch, that hurts," cried Jenny as one of the men tightened the rope around her arms.

"Shut up, you brat!" he said. "You heard the boss. And, believe me, if any of you think of trying to escape, we'll just finish you off right then. Do you understand? You got us in a lot of hot water with the boss, and I would love to have the chance to get even with you!"

As they finally finished tying up the last one, a knock came at the door, and a nervous-looking man entered.

"Ching," said one of the men curtly, "the boss said for you to guard these kids and make sure they don't escape. If anything happens to them, it's curtains for you and us! Do you understand?"

"I understand," Ching replied in a frightened voice. "I'll guard them with my life."

"Ha! You better, you idiot! You know what the boss thinks of you already," they snarled as they left.

The cabin door closed behind the men, and the four youngsters watched Ching curiously. He seemed to be in about as much trouble as they were. They all wondered why he seemed so frightened.

No one said a word. Ching inspected the ropes which held the four securely in their chairs. Then, to their surprise, he spoke to them in English.

"Who are you kids, and what are you doing here anyway? Do you know you are in trouble with one of the meanest men I've ever met?" he asked. "My advice to you is that you don't try any monkey business with him if you ever expect to be free again!"

Ching's sympathetic tone and his speaking English brought a ray of hope and helped the youngsters relax a bit. Ching seemed different than the other captors. He even seemed a little bit friendly. They prayed more earnestly for wisdom and help.

Encouraged by Ching's remarks, Tim began to explain their plight. "Really, Ching," he said, "we didn't mean to do anything wrong. We were just exploring around the temple and discovered the car under the rice stalks in the barn. Those men returned unexpectedly, and we hid behind the stalks. We overheard them talking about the armored truck robbery and realized the car fit the police description of one of the vehicles used in the robbery."

"What armored truck robbery are you talking about?" asked Ching in surprise.

Jack filled him in because he obviously knew nothing about the robbery. Ching was shocked and began to wring his hands in agitation.

"Now, I'm really in trouble," he said with obvious fear. "I never should have gone to that gambling house! They're a bunch of bank robbers and kidnappers, too! And, I work for the boss!"

Ching seemed anxious to share his story. "My luck was really bad that night and I lost everything I had--and then some! Since I couldn't pay up, the man they call the boss said I could pay off my debt by working on his launch, but I'm really a prisoner here," he explained. "They watch me all the time and constantly threaten me with death. I'm afraid I'll never get free because I know too much about their wicked schemes. And now this robbery and the kidnapping of you children! They are a bunch of criminals, and I'll be implicated by just being here. But you've got to believe me. I am not one of them. I gambled and lost, and now I'm in a lot of trouble."

The ropes were cutting into Jenny's arms causing her a lot of pain, but she was intrigued with Ching's story. *Maybe God has a plan for our escape,* she thought.

"Oh, Ching," she said. "That means all of us are in trouble with the boss. I thought you were one of the robbers. I'm sure glad to know you are not one of them."

The others responded in agreement, realizing instinctively that Ching might be able to help them.

"I'm not one of them for sure," he replied emphatically, "but I sure am in a mess."

Jack chose his words carefully as he spoke, "Ching, we got ourselves into this mess by snooping around the barn when we should have stayed out of other people's property. We really didn't mean to do anything wrong. We were just curious."

Ching didn't respond, so Jack continued. "Since we were discovered, we've been praying that God would send someone to help us before it is too late. You see, we are all Christians, and we believe God answers prayer. We have been asking Him to send someone to help us. You know what I think? Maybe you're that someone!"

"Me?" Ching asked in astonishment, "How could I help you? And besides, why should I? You heard what those men said. If I help you in any way, I would be a dead man! Uh, uh! No sir! I wouldn't dare help you."

"But we're just kids!" Ruth said desperately. "Do you have any kids of your own, Ching? Wouldn't you want someone to help them if they were in trouble?"

Now it was Ching's turn to be shocked and speechless. "Better stop the talking and be quiet," he said softly. "Someone may hear us."

Everyone lapsed into silence after that, but in their hearts the four friends prayed fervently that somehow Ching would help them out of the predicament. They realized all five of them were in deep trouble, and only God could save them now. And they wondered what the boss had in mind for them.

Jack figured in the morning when the tide rose, the cruiser would take off, and the robbers would dispose of them at sea. *They'll probably stuff us in weighted bags and dump us overboard,* he thought. *No one would ever find us. Mom and Dad would never know what happened to us!*

Time passed slowly as Ching sat there quietly. He eyed the four kids furtively from time to time and wondered to himself, *how can they look so calm in the face of such a terrible situation*? He thought about his own children at home. He hadn't seen them for weeks. They knew he was "working" on the cruiser, but not even his wife knew the whole story. He was afraid to tell her lest she call the police and make things worse for him. But he desperately wanted to be free and reunited with his family. He promised himself that if he ever got free, he would never gamble again!

"It's all my fault," Jenny whispered to Ruth in a quivering voice, "Why did I have to sneeze? Oh Ruth, I'm so sorry I got you into all this trouble."

"It's not your fault, Jenny. We're all in this together, so don't blame yourself," Ruth whispered, trying to sound brave. "Remember that verse in the Bible that says, 'All things work together for good to them that love the Lord?'"

"Yes, I remember that, and .... ," she paused and quickly added , "and I believe it!" she said resolutely.

Ching was roused from his thoughts by the girls' whispering.

"Hey, didn't I tell you to be quiet?" he asked sharply.

The girls were frightened, and the boys shot them warning glances, but Jenny summoned up all the courage left in her and replied softly, "I just told Ruth all of this mess was my fault. When we were hiding under the rice stalks, I sneezed, and we were discovered. I just asked her to forgive me for getting her into trouble."

"What kind of kids are you, anyway?" asked Ching, looking from one to the other in amazement. "You say you pray to God to send someone to help you, and you ask forgiveness of one another? I've never met any kids like you before. And you said you were Christians! I can't figure that one out. Two of you are Chinese, and two of you are foreigners, but all Christians? How can that be?"

Tim spoke up and told Ching how he and Ruth came from a Buddhist family, but had given their lives to Jesus Christ and found forgiveness of their sins and new peace in their hearts.

"I know the dangerous circumstances you are in and how close to death you are," Ching said. "How can you be so calm and unafraid? Why I'm scared almost out of my wits. I'm afraid of dying because I don't know what will happen to me after that!"

"Ching, we're scared too, but we have found hope in Jesus Christ, our Savior," said Jack. "And like Tim said, if we should be killed, we would go to heaven to be with Jesus. That's the reason we can be calm. But more than that, we believe God is going to send us help somehow and answer our prayers."

Jack spoke with such confidence that Ching listened attentively although it was hard for him to believe anyone could speak so calmly in such a dangerous situation.

Jack was encouraged by Ching's attention. "You can have that same peace in your heart by trusting in Jesus, just as we have," he said.

At that point Ching changed the subject, turned to the girls and said, “Are those ropes cutting into your wrists? Maybe I could loosen them a little and make you more comfortable. I can’t take them off, but I can at least ease the pain.”

Without waiting for an answer, he proceeded to loosen all their ropes. What a relief for everyone as their blood began circulating in their arms again.

Encouraged by this unexpected act of kindness, Jack picked up the conversation. “You know, Ching, when the police capture this gang, you’re going to be in as much trouble as the rest of them, especially since you’re guarding us. What would you think about doing something to prove that you’re innocent?”

“What do you mean by that?” Ching asked with interest. “How could I prove to anyone that I am innocent?”

"Well, you could help us escape." replied Jack. "If we make it, we would testify on your behalf. Any judge would believe your story."

There was a long silence again as Ching mulled these ideas over in his mind. Everyone was feeling tired from the long chase and lack of sleep, but they were busy praying that God would intervene and cause Ching to consider helping them escape.

Chapter 11

Escape in the Dinghy

The silence seemed to last forever, but no one dared interrupt Ching's thoughts. They knew he was considering Jack's proposition, so they just prayed and waited. Then Ching looked at the children with new warmth in his eyes. When he spoke, there was a lilt in his voice.

"I've been a fool, and I've made a mess of my life. But you kids say I could really do something to help you and, maybe in the process, make up for all my past failures. You may be right! I've been thinking of an escape plan."

Four heads popped up at the words '*I've been thinking of an escape plan.*'

"Really, Ching?" exclaimed Jack in surprise. "Are you really thinking of a plan to help us escape?"

"You all started me thinking this evening. If I expect to make something of my life, I better get on the right side! Right?"

"Right!" they all chimed in together.

"So what's the plan, Ching? "asked Tim.

"Well, there's a chance I could help you girls get in the dinghy tied up at the gangway. Then you could row over to the launch anchored about a quarter of a mile away and get help. Do you know how to row a boat?"

"Oh, no!" sighed Ruth in dismay. "I've never been in a dinghy. I wouldn't know the first thing about how to row one!"

"That's no problem," chimed in Jenny with a big smile. "I've been rowing several times. I'm sure I could do it! Besides, we don't have any choice, do we?"

They all began to talk at once, getting energized and hopeful, thinking about the escape.

"Wait a minute! Wait a minute!" responded Ching with a low chuckle. "We've got to be quiet or someone may get suspicious. I didn't say it would work, but it might be worth a try. It will be dangerous, but if we stay here, we'll all be killed for sure. On the other hand, if we could somehow summon the police, there is a chance we could all come out of this alive."

"I think I ought to go," said Jack emphatically. "I'm the oldest, and I've done a lot of rowing. It is too dangerous and difficult for the girls. I wouldn't want them to be in that kind of danger."

"That's very brave of you," replied Ching, "but if it was discovered you were missing, it could go very bad for the girls here. These men are capable of doing anything. I don't think you would want to expose them to that kind of danger, now would you?"

"You're right," Jack replied thoughtfully. "I never thought of that." Tell us more about your plan. There isn't much time left."

"Okay, here is my suggestion. The little dinghy is tied to the gangway. It has a small motor on it, but the noise of the engine would alert the others and ruin the plan for escape. So you have to use the emergency oars attached to the sides of the boat. It will be slower and difficult to row, but it might just make the escape possible. We men will have to take the consequences here and just hope that we'll be rescued."

"Right on, Ching," said Tim with enthusiasm. "Let's get started right away. I'm sure the Lord will help us and send someone to rescue all of us."

"Right," added Jack excitedly, "but first, let's pray together and ask the Lord to help us with this plan."

Jack led the group in a simple prayer, asking for protection. He prayed especially for Ching to come to understand God's love for him. Then he thanked the Lord for answering prayer and for watching over them. Everyone joined in a hearty 'amen.' Now they were ready for action.

"Now, I'll go outside and make sure everyone is asleep," said Ching. "If the way is clear, we'll get the girls in the boat and see how lucky we are."

"That sounds good, Ching," said Jack, "except we don't believe in luck. We believe in God who works miracles for His praying children."

"Well, whatever," said Ching a little defensively. "I don't know your God, but if this works, I want to find out more about Him."

Ching quietly slipped out of the cabin and stealthily walked around the deck. Everyone seemed to be asleep. All the lights were out in the cabins, so he returned and told them the way was clear. Then he untied the ropes binding them to the chairs. It took a few minutes before the circulation returned to their arms and legs.

"Now comes the dangerous part," said Ching. "Girls, follow me as quietly as possible. One misstep and we'll be discovered. That would be the end for all of us. I'll lead you to the gangway. It's still lowered. Walk carefully down the steps and get into the dinghy. After you untie the ropes, immediately push away from the side of the boat to get out of the glare of the gangway lights. The current is quite strong, and that will cause you to drift away from the boat and into the darkness. Next, feel along the sides of the boat until you locate the oars. You must put them into the sockets so you can row. Then, head for the closest launch. When you get there, tie up to the gangway and wake up the people. Tell them to call the harbor police. Tell them to get here as soon as possible. Do you understand all of that?"

"Yes we do," replied Jenny. "Now just pray that we can make it quickly."

"Good," said Ching. "Now you fellows sit tight and don't make a sound. Okay, here goes!"

He quietly opened the door, carefully stuck out his head and looked in both directions. Then he motioned for the girls to follow. Jack closed the door, and then they prayed for God's special help for the girls. At the gangway, Ching motioned the girls to go ahead. They cautiously crept down the gangway, holding their breath each time they stepped on a creaky board. Finally, they reached the boat at the bottom. *So far, so good,* thought Jenny as she began untying the ropes. The current was swift, like Ching had said, and it pulled the dinghy away from the boat, out into the darkness. Ching hurried back to the cabin and locked the door. The girls began feeling for the oars. Finding them wasn't easy in the darkness.

"Here's one of them," exclaimed Ruth excitedly.

"Good! And here's the other one!" whispered Jenny as she set them into their sockets. Soon she had the dinghy turned and headed in the right direction. The tide was beginning to come in which made it difficult to stay on course, but as the lights of the Twin Dragon receded, the girls were encouraged. They were going to make it!

"Jenny, it's working!" said Ruth hardly daring to hope. "I'm praying this will work!"

"So am I. Just keep me headed in the right direction. This tide keeps pulling us off course. "Oh, Lord Jesus," Jenny prayed, "help us reach that launch and get help! I'm exhausted. Unless you help me, I don't think I can pull against this tide."

"You're doing great, Jenny," Ruth encouraged. "Pull on the right oar a little. A little more. There, that's good. We're headed straight for the launch. It looks like the gangway is on this side. Oh, Jenny, I just know the Lord is helping us!"

****

Meanwhile, back on the Twin Dragon, the men were beginning to stir. The boss had instructed them to weigh anchor at about 5:00 a.m. and head out to sea. It was now 4:30 a.m., and the first rays of dawn were beginning to break in the eastern sky.

"Raise the gangway and get the dinghy on board," said the boss. "Some of you men get the fishing tackle out and in place, so we'll look like we're leaving on a fishing trip. Make sure the poles are in place when we pass the lighthouse and report our departure. We've got to make this look good."

"Just as you say, boss," said the sailor in charge. "We'll be ready to shove off at 5:00 a.m."

****

A half mile away, the dinghy was slowly approaching the launch. As soon as the gangway was within reach, Ruth started tying up. They clambered up the gangway, calling out loudly as they climbed the swaying steps.

"Help! Help! Wake up! Please, somebody help us!" they called as they reached the top.

The startled couple on board came out on deck, rubbing the sleep out of their eyes. Seeing the two girls, the surprised owner began asking questions. "Who are you? What are you doing on our launch? How did you get here?"

Breathlessly, the girls poured out their story. Pointing to the Twin Dragon, they pleaded, "Oh, please, quick! Call the harbor police! You've got to call the harbor police to rescue our brothers and Ching!"

The owner wasted no time rushing the girls to the radio room. Still dazed from being awakened so abruptly at this early hour, he nevertheless reacted quickly and reached the harbor patrol. "Is this the harbor patrol?" he asked with tension filling his voice. "My name is Reney, and I'm on board the launch Marguerite anchored at buoy number 27. I have two girls here who say they escaped from the Twin Dragon at number 28. They say the men on the launch kidnapped them yesterday and are planning to kill them!"

"Great," replied the officer excitedly. "We've been searching for two girls since last night. Any chance their names are Jenny Carlton and Ruth Chen?"

"I don't know. Let me ask them." Turning to the two girls he asked, "Are you Jenny Carlton and Ruth Chen?"

"Yes, we were kidnapped in the New Territories yesterday and brought out to the Twin Dragon last night," Jenny said.

After Mr. Reney confirmed who the girls were, the officer replied, "Terrific! We've been searching everywhere for them. Take care of them and leave the rest to us."

****

In a few minutes, the phone in the hotel jarred the Carltons and the Chens awake. They had fallen into fitful sleep after waiting all night for word from the police. Mr. Carlton jumped to the phone.

"Hello! Hello!" he cried excitedly. "This is the Carltons. Who is this?"

"Mr. Carlton," came the reply. "This is the Hong Kong police. We have located your children!"

Mr. Carlton shouted to the others. "They've found the children!" The others came scrambling to the phone.

"Are they all right?" Mr. Carlton asked.

"The girls are okay. We know where they are, but I'm sorry to say the boys are still in grave danger," continued the officer. "The girls made it safely to another boat nearby and called for help."

"They're on a boat? How did they get there?" Mr. Carlton asked as hundreds of questions filled his mind.

The officer continued to explain as much as he knew and told the parents to stand by and wait for further word. They would do their very best to capture the kidnappers and set the boys free.

"We'll call as soon as we have more word. Don't worry we're already underway."

Pandemonium broke loose in the Carlton's hotel room.

"Oh, praise the Lord!" said Mr. Carlton. "God is answering our prayers. But the boys are still in danger. We need to pray for their safety."

"Oh, please do that right away," begged Mrs. Chen anxiously. "Now I know God is alive and answers prayer. I'm ready to follow the children in becoming a Christian," she boldly confessed. She turned to her husband wondering what his response would be. He just sat there stunned and mumbled that all he wanted right now was the safe return of the four children.

Mr. Carlton prayed and thanked God for the good news. He prayed earnestly for the safety and return of the children. Then he thanked God that Mrs. Chen had made the important decision to follow Jesus!

Chapter 12

The Escape Discovered

Back on board the Twin Dragon, commotion broke out when a sailor discovered the dinghy was missing. He rushed back to the boss, shouting at the top of his voice, "The dinghy's missing! There's no sign of it anywhere!"

"What do you mean, the dinghy's missing?" shouted the boss. "How could that be? Did anyone leave the ship? Answer me!" he continued shouting fiercely at his petrified men.

"Check on the prisoners you idiots. Hurry!" he ranted as he rushed out on deck toward the cabin where the prisoners were being held.

Pounding on the door, he shouted to Ching to open the door! Ching realized someone had discovered the missing dinghy.

"Quick," he whispered to Jack and Tim, "get into that closet over there and don't come out. There may be some shooting, so lie low. Don't make a sound, not even if they discover me! The boss is a mean man and he's ready to kill!"

The boss and his men were pounding insistently on the door and shouting vile oaths at Ching. Ching quickly pushed the boys into the closet. Then he decided the best thing for him to do was to hide there also. Fortunately, he had a key to lock the closet door. That would delay their discovery a little longer. He had no way of knowing whether or not the girls had reached the launch. He was hoping that they did and that help would be on the way soon.

"That's a strong lock on the cabin door," he said to the boys. "They won't break it off very easily. We need all the time possible for the police to get here."

"Here, stand aside," one man yelled. "We can break it open with this ax. Let me at it!"

The boss was furious and continued to shout at the top of his voice for Ching to open the door or suffer the consequences!

The door was really a strong one, and even though the man with the ax was very skillful, it didn't yield very easily. Finally, the door splintered and cracked as three of the men pounded it with their full weight.

"My plan's working," Ching said happily. "That's a stout door, and it is slowing them down. Maybe the police will make it in time."

Unknown to Ching and the boys, two speedy patrol boats were already underway, and the police helicopter was being ordered aloft.

The cabin door finally yielded to the full weight of the men. It swung crazily on its hinges as the men fell headlong into the room. There was no sign of anyone. The only thing they saw were four empty chairs and the ropes laying on the floor.

"They've all escaped!" shouted the bewildered men. "No telling where they are now. They will be calling the police! What are we to do now?"

The boss was angry as a hornet. He stormed out of the room, barking orders to head out to sea immediately.

"We'll make a run for Macau," he bellowed. "It's only 40 miles from here. If we're lucky we'll reach it before the police catch up to us. Hurry up! Get those engines started. We don't have any time to lose!"

He rushed to the bridge to supervise the escape. Every man on board turned his attention to getting out to international waters ahead of the police. In a matter of minutes the launch was underway and gliding swiftly towards the port entrance. The boss was very angry and agitated and made terrible threats to the two men who had left the barn door open.

As the Twin Dragon moved out to sea, it passed within shouting distance of the Marguerite.

"We're moving," Ching announced. "They're making a run for it. That means Jenny and Ruth must have made it to the other launch!"

Jack and Tim, who were still hiding in the closet with Ching, had no way of knowing that Jenny and Ruth were on the bridge watching the launch as it passed.

"There they go!" shouted Jenny. "They're heading out to sea! Oh, Mr. Reney, do something!"

"We have done everything we can at this moment," Mr. Reney said. "But let me call the police again and tell them the Twin Dragon is headed out of the harbor. I'm sure they'll intercept them at the mouth of the harbor."

In a few moments he had the police on the radio again. "The Twin Dragon just passed us on its way out to sea," he reported. "Hurry!"

The girls heard the police officer reply over the speaker, "Everything's under control, Mr. Reney. Two boats are on the way to intercept them, and we'll soon have a police helicopter in the air. Hopefully, it won't be long before we have them in custody."

The girls sighed with relief.

"You girls look exhausted. You better come and have some hot chocolate," Mr. Reney said. "My wife has it all ready. You need some nourishment after that long rowing trip. You were brave girls to venture out in the dark like that. Your parents must be very proud of you."

Just then, the radio phone rang.

"Yes, that's right," said Mr. Reney. "The two girls are right here, having hot chocolate. They rowed over to our launch to tell us about the kidnappers. Don't worry, the police are hot on the trail of the kidnappers right this minute."

He paused, turned to Jenny and said, "It's your father. He wants to talk with you."

Jenny jumped up and took the phone excitedly. "Dad!" she cried, "we're okay. The people on this launch have been helping us. The Twin Dragon just passed us, but the police say they expect to capture it very soon. Keep praying for the boys."

After both girls had talked with their parents, they settled down to wait for the report. *Will the police get there in time?* they wondered. They shuddered to think what would happen to Jack and Tim if they didn't.

****

Meanwhile, on board the Twin Dragon the boss was fussing and fuming, urging his engineer to go faster. Pacing back and forth, he kept searching the waters all around them for any sign of the harbor police. He had a sinking feeling in his stomach that they were in deep trouble.

It was twelve miles before they would reach international waters and freedom! Daylight was breaking fast on the sleepy harbor, and many little boats were already moving about. The Twin Dragon was on a straight course to the harbor entrance. It would be too bad if any small boat got in the way! He was intent on escaping, no matter what.

Suddenly he was startled by a sailor who shouted, "Police boats approaching on the port side!"

The boss cursed as he turned and saw the boats in the distance.

"Faster!" he yelled. "We've got to make it to the open sea!"

Just then he heard the drone of the approaching helicopter. Searching the sky, he saw the police helicopter rapidly overtaking them. The other gang members panicked as the police trap closed in on them. The boss took his powerful rifle from the rack and stood defiantly, as if to challenge the whole police department.

"Don't slacken your speed or I'll shoot you," he ordered the man at the pilot wheel.

"Keep going! We can outrun them! Grab your guns and hold them off. Once we get out to sea, we can make our escape," he shouted at his men.

In the cabin closet, Ching and the boys huddled together silently. They felt the throb of the engines and knew the launch was moving rapidly. Hearing the shouting going on outside, they also knew that something was up, but they didn't know whether to be fearful or hopeful.

"What do you think is happening?" asked Jack.

"I don't know for sure," Ching answered hopefully, "but I think the girls reached the launch, and the police are coming. Listen, that sounds like a helicopter approaching. I think the rescue is underway!"

"You're right!" said Tim excitedly. "It must be a police helicopter! That means the harbor patrol must be close by, too! This is it, fellows! We will soon be rescued."

"The boss won't give up without a fight," said Jack, "but this really is a miracle. God heard our prayers, and I know we will soon be free."

Just as he said that, they heard the sharp crack of a rifle and then more shots.

"They're going to fight it out with the police," Ching said. "The boss is a desperate man. He'll fight to the finish."

"What should we do?" asked Jack with a tremor in his voice. "If we stay here and the gun battle continues, this boat might be blown up!"

"None of the men are concerned with us right now," replied Ching. "There are some life preservers nearby. I'll see if I can get them. We may have to jump overboard and swim to safety. Can you boys swim?"

Assured that they could, he slipped out of the closet while sporadic shooting continued. Then he heard a loud speaker from the police launch ordering them to cease firing and surrender. That was met with a volley of shots. The helicopter hovered overhead. Still the Twin Dragon didn't slow down. It was making a wild dash for the open sea!

Ching was able to get three of the inflatable life preservers without being discovered. Everyone was concentrating on the police launches and the fight they had on their hands. The noise of gun shots and the loud speakers continued as the launch was churning up a powerful wake behind as it wove back and forth in a wild attempt to avoid the police.

Ching helped the boys put their life jackets on and told them what to do if they had to go overboard. He was also keeping a sharp eye on the activities going on around them.

"Boys, I think the best thing for us to do is to jump overboard and swim to the nearest boat," he said. "If we stay here, we will be trapped in a real shoot-out which may cause a fire on board. While everyone is so busy holding off the police, we can jump overboard safely. What do you say? Are you game for that?"

"Sure thing, Ching," the boys said. "If we stay here, we'll be caught in the crossfire, and there's no telling what will happen to us."

"God has already answered our prayers and helped the girls. Now He will help us, too," Jack said reassuringly.

"Okay then," said Ching, "when I give the signal, run as fast as you can, and jump over the rail. Swim under water as long as you can and get as far away as possible from the boat before surfacing. These men may take pot shots at us if they see us go overboard, but the boat is going so fast, we will soon be out of their range. Now, let me take a look and see what's happening."

As Ching carefully stuck his head out of the doorway, the two boys prayed silently and thanked God for helping the girls alert the police.

Ching turned to the boys, "Everyone's at the stern holding off the police launches. Our best bet is to run out and jump overboard. Let's see, are those jackets on right? Remember—swim under water as long as you can. Then pull the cord to inflate the life jacket, and you'll surface quickly. Got it?"

"Got it," the boys responded.

"Okay, we're all set. Let's go!"

With that, Ching led the way with the boys right behind. As they rushed out, he helped them over the rail. Both went flying through the air and hit the water with a splash. Then he jumped. At that moment, the boss caught a glimpse of them escaping. He trained his rifle on Ching. Just as he hit the water, he felt a sting in his right arm. He'd been hit! The rush of cold water numbed the pain. All he could do was use his left arm to swim underwater away from the ship.

He dared not come up yet—he might still be in range of the kidnappers' guns. When he couldn't hold his breath any longer, he inflated his life preserver which pulled him to the surface. He gulped in the fresh air. The launch had passed him, and everyone on board was more engaged with the police than with him. He looked around. *Where are the boys?* Then he saw their heads bobbing in the water some distance away. They made it, too. They were all safe!

The gun battle had attracted several small boats in the area. They cautiously followed at a safe distance. Seeing three people jump overboard, they approached the swimmers slowly. No one could be sure who they were or why they had jumped. The boys yelled for help. When the men in the small fishing boat saw they were young boys, they pulled alongside and hauled Jack and Tim on board. Everyone was talking excitedly and asking Tim all kinds of questions.

Meanwhile, Ching was struggling to swim toward a nearby boat, but it was slow going, His right arm was useless for swimming. I'm losing a lot of blood, he thought. I need help as soon as possible. "Over here. Help!" he yelled. "I'm wounded."

The men lifted him as gently as possible into their boat. "Get the first-aid kit. Quick!"

While they bandaged his wound, he asked, "What about the two boys? Are they safe?"

"That boat over there picked up two people," replied the captain. "They're okay, I think. What's this all about?"

Ching briefly described their escape from the kidnappers and asked them to take him back to shore immediately. The fishing boat had already turned and was headed back to shore.

On the Marguerite, the girls and the Reneys watched the chase. They had no idea that the boys had jumped overboard in the distance and knew only that there was lots of action going on out there.

"Now," said Mr. Reney, "suppose we head to shore. We will want to be on hand when your brothers come in with the police."

"Oh, that would be great!" replied Jenny excitedly. "I just hope they will be rescued quickly."

"If I know anything about the Hong Kong police," replied Mr. Reney, "it won't be long until they are safe and sound and back on land. Let's go!"

But at that moment, it was anything but safe around the Twin Dragon. A third police launch was now approaching from the harbor entrance. The Twin Dragon was hemmed in, and the helicopter was hovering overhead forcing the ship to stop. The police ordered the kidnappers to lay down their weapons and surrender.

The frightened crew members threw down their guns, but the boss was defiant and continued firing at the police. At last, realizing how desperate his situation was, he jumped overboard and attempted to escape detection. It was a hopeless attempt, because the police immediately pulled alongside, hauled him aboard and placed him in hand-cuffs. He was a sorry looking sight with his hair plastered down on his face and his wet clothes clinging to his body—quite different from the snarling, dapper man of the night before.

The police boarded the Twin Dragon and placed everyone on board under arrest. With the crew in handcuffs, they started the search for the boys. When the search failed to produce Jack and Tim, they radioed to shore that the launch was captured, but there was no sign of the boys.

Chapter 13

Safe at Last

The boys scrambled off the fishing boat and were welcomed by the police waiting on shore.

"Are you guys okay?" inquired an anxious officer.

"We're okay," gasped the boys. "Did anyone see a man in the water? His name is Ching."

"You're the first ashore," replied the officer. "Who's this fellow Ching?"

Tim explained how Ching had rescued them from the robbers and jumped over the side with them.

"Here comes another boat," said the officer. "There's a man on board, and he's got some bandages on his arm. That must be Ching."

Just then, Jenny and Ruth came rushing towards Tim and Jack. What a reunion they had! After hugging them tightly the girls were soon almost as wet as the boys.

"What happened to Ching?" they asked.

"The last I saw of him was when he helped me jump overboard," said Jack. "Look, isn't that him being carried out on a stretcher? He must have been hurt!"

"That's him all right!" shouted Tim. "Let's go over and see him. I sure hope it's not serious."

All four children rushed over just as Ching was being lifted off the fishing boat. The medics carried him off the boat to the waiting ambulance. Rushing up, they tried to reach him with a happy welcome, but a police officer held them back.

"This man is under arrest. Stand back!" the police shouted.

There was a chorus of protests from all four as they tried to explain to the police that this man had rescued them. He was their friend.

"Oh, Ching," called Jenny as the police held them back. "Are you hurt badly?"

"I'll be okay," he called reassuringly. "I only took a shot to my arm. I was really lucky."

The police were intrigued with the welcome Ching received from the children.

"What's going on here?" an officer asked in surprise. "Isn't this man one of the kidnappers? Do you know him?"

"We sure do," said Jack with a big grin on his face. "If it hadn't been for this man, we wouldn't be alive right now. He saved us!"

Jack tried to tell the story while Jenny, Tim and Ruth kept interjecting comments in favor of Ching.

"That may all be true," said the officer, "but he was on board that launch, and we have to arrest him. As far as we know, he's one of the kidnappers."

"Oh, no!" Jenny cried. "He's not a kidnapper. He's our friend! Believe me, he saved our lives!"

"We'll hear the whole story later and let the judge decide," replied the officer. "We'll take good care of him. Don't worry about that. First, we'll get him to a hospital and get his arm taken care of."

Ching was being loaded into the waiting ambulance, but he smiled at his new friends and called, "I'll be okay, kids. Don't worry about me. I'll be okay. Come and see me if you can. But please tell the police the whole story. I'm counting on you!"

"We sure will," they called to him. "We'll bring our folks to meet you!"

The police officers were amazed at the reception the wounded man received and wondered what it was all about. Nevertheless, they had to place Ching under medical arrest.

"We better get back to the police station and get the whole story," said the friendly police officer. "Your folks will be arriving soon. They are very anxious to see you. You helped us capture some pretty big thieves today, so I suspect a lot of newspaper reporters will be there also. This is big news."

As the kids piled into the police cruiser for the trip to the station, each one said a prayer and thanked the Lord for saving them.

At the station the Carltons and the Chens came rushing in, grabbed their kids and gave them big hugs. What a relief to have them returned safely!

Everyone was surprised when Captain Ling walked in. "My, my," he said. "You kids have a special knack for catching big thieves! I wonder what's going to happen the next time you come to Hong Kong."

The mothers looked at each other and with a smile, Mrs. Carlton replied, "We're going to keep them under house arrest if we come back again!"

Everyone laughed as they continued hugging each other.

"Say, we better get you kids home and into some dry clothes," said Mr. Carlton. "Then we can celebrate with a family meal."

The lead story on the late morning news was a full report of the girls' heroism in rowing to the Marguerite to get help. The story of the daring rescue had complete coverage, and the police were praised highly for rescuing the four young people so quickly. There was also a story about Ching. When he was interviewed at the hospital, he just lay there smiling. All he had to say was praise for his four new friends. The whole story—his involvement with the gang and how the children had verified his heroic actions in helping them escape—came out in the report.

"I think the judge will be very lenient on Ching," said Captain Ling as he sat with the Carltons and the Chens. "He seems to have a very plausible story, and you kids backed up every word of it. It is obvious he was not part of that evil gang."

"That's right, Captain," said Jack. "He is a very brave man who risked his life for us. We will all testify to that and hope the judge will let him return to his family."

The news report continued, saying the police had recovered all the money after following the children's directions to the hiding place. The bank had offered a reward of $3,000 dollars for any information leading to the discovery of the stolen money from the armored car, so the money would be split between the four children for their heroic part in the robbers' arrest.

"Hey, Mom!" Jack shouted to his mother in the kitchen. "Did you hear that? We're going to get the $3,000 reward for finding the money!"

"Three thousand dollars!" she exclaimed. "For you?"

"It will be split between the four of you kids. That's what the reporter says," chimed in Mr. Chen who was beaming from ear to ear with pride.

"Well, that will be a good start on my college fund. Wow! Can you believe that? See Mom, it pays to chase down robbers, don't you think?" Jack said with a sly grin on his face.

"I can think of better ways to earn money for college," she replied with a smile as she hugged him.

The other three were talking about their share of the reward and agreed most of their money would go toward their college education.

The women went back to set the table for breakfast while the men continued chatting about the excitement of the past 24 hours. When Mrs. Carlton came back to call them to eat, the three men put their fingers to their lips and pointed to the four youngsters sound asleep in their chairs—totally exhausted from their high adventure.

Chapter 14

Parting News

The next few days sped by, and soon it was time for the Carltons to return home. The parting was made easier with the news that Mrs. Chen had prayed to receive the Lord as her Savior after the children were kidnapped. The twins rejoiced with Tim and Ruth about their mother's decision. Now their father was the only one who had not yet made a decision.

"But he is very close," said Tim. "The other night he remarked that this is the first time in his life he ever experienced an answer to prayer. Still, he said he had to remain a Buddhist to take care of his ancestors. I believe he will make his own decision one of these days though. Then our whole family will be Christians. Keep on praying for this to happen and for us to live as true Christians before him."

"Not a single day passes that we don't pray for your family," Jenny replied. "These visits have been the most wonderful experiences of our lives."

"And we will be looking forward to seeing you again soon," chimed in Jack. "I wonder where that will be, and what will happen then?"

"Well, smugglers and bank robbers are very exciting," replied Tim, "but the best part of these summers has been your leading us to know Jesus. That is the best thing that ever happened to our family. We will never stop thanking God for that."

Several weeks after the Carltons returned to the States, the kidnappers' trial took place. They were all given long prison sentences—all but Ching. When the whole story was told, the boss finally confessed that Ching had nothing to do with the robbery and didn't even know anything about it. The judge set him free, and he was reunited with his family. Mr. Chen was able to help him find a new job in the company warehouse which enabled him to provide for his family.

Tim and Ruth also kept in contact with him and kept urging him to bring his family to church. Although Christianity was all new to him, Ching was very responsive to them. As soon as he was freed, he and his family started attending church.

The Carltons eagerly read each letter from the Chens, and they all thanked God the judge gave Ching another chance. They thanked God too, that he was seeking new life in Jesus Christ. Their constant prayer was that Ching and his family would all receive Christ into their hearts. What a perfect ending to their second trip to Hong Kong.

One day, Tim and Ruth were discussing the events of the past year. "Just think," Tim said, "if the Carltons had not come to Hong Kong, we would not be Christians today! Jack and Jenny have been faithful witnesses for the Lord and helped us find our way to Him."

"That's right," said Ruth. "And remember, Mom has also become a Christian and Captain Ling and his family are back in church. And then there's Ching. I can hardly believe all this has happened just because Jack and Jenny were faithful in serving the Lord. I want to follow their example and win as many as possible to Jesus.

"That's the truth for sure," replied Tim with real enthusiasm. "It just shows how young people can do great things for God when they are willing. I believe that if we are just as faithful to the Lord, Dad will make his decision someday."

Mrs. Chen overheard their conversation and added, "You're right, children. I'm a believer today because of your faithfulness in telling me about Jesus. Now we're going to concentrate our prayers on Dad. Some day, I believe he will become a believer, too."

And with a twinkle in her eyes she added, "But let's pray that he will come to the Lord without another scary experience!"

"But Mom," protested Tim, "discovering how God answers prayer was what brought us to believe in Him. And since God watched over us in these two scary situations, I think we can trust Him for anything in the future."

The End

Would you like to know Jesus?

Jack and Jenny went through some difficult situations. But even when it was hard, they still prayed and trusted in Jesus. He doesn't always take us out of the tough times, but He walks with us through them. Do you know Jesus as your Savior?

In the Bible, God tells us that we all have sinned. Think about the ten commandments which are God's standard for our lives. One of them says that we should not lie. I think we all have lied. Another says that you should not murder. Now, of course, you haven't murdered anyone, but Jesus says that if we hate someone, that is the same as murder. Wow! We all fail the test. BUT the good news is that Jesus Christ came to earth as a man, lived a sinless life among us, died on the cross for our sins (even lying and hatred), and then He rose again to break the power of sin. Because of Jesus, we are now able to be part of the family of God. And He will walk with us, helping us to live our lives for Him, just like Jack and Jenny trusted in Jesus.

If you want to believe that Jesus is the Savior as He says He is, then you can pray the following prayer:

Dear Lord Jesus, I need you as my Savior and Lord. I thank You for dying on the cross for my sin. I now open the door of my heart and receive You as my Savior. Thank you for forgiving me of all my sin and giving me eternal life. Help me to live as a Christian ought to live according to Your Word, the Bible. In Jesus' name, Amen.

Talk to your parents about this and tell them what you did. If you would like to write to tell me about your decision, or if you have any questions or comments you can reach me at my email address agbollback@churchinchina.com. May God bless you!

About the Author

Anthony Bollback was born into a Christian home that always entertained missionaries. He received Christ at age 16 after a near-drowning incident at Old Orchard Beach, Maine. Beginning his missionary career in China, he and his wife Evelyn, were forced to evacuate when the Communists took over, and two years later began serving in Japan for five years. The remainder of his 24 years in Asia was spent in Hong Kong where he planted and directed 10 chapels and schools with 10,000 students. He served as Field Chairman of the China-Hong Kong Field of The Christian and Missionary Alliance for four years. Unexpectedly, God changed his direction and sent him to Honolulu for a most effective ministry as pastor of Kapahulu Bible Church. He retired from active ministry after serving as District Superintendent of the Mid-America District C&MA for 9 very productive years. Following retirement to Florida, he actively began a writing career and the publishing of 12 books.

Books by Anthony Bollback

Jack and Jenny Mystery Series

Smugglers in Hong Kong
Capture of the Twin Dragon
Mystery of the Counterfeit Money
Rescue at Cripple Creek
The Tiger Shark Strikes Again
Hijacked

Other Books by Anthony Bollback

To China and Back--autobiography
Red Runs the River: historical fiction of the persecuted church in China, Volume 1
Exiles of Hope: historical fiction of the persecuted church in China, Volume 2
Surprised by God: five years of miracles in Japan after evacuating from China

CPSIA information can be obtained at www.ICGtesting.com
Printed in the USA
BVOW030853070512

289401BV00001B/9/P